Guide Dogs

Abigail Richter

Rosen REAL READERS

The Rosen Publishing Group, Inc.
New York

Guide dogs help people who cannot see.

Puppies are born in schools for guide dogs.

The puppies live with families to learn many new things.

The puppies get used to people touching them.

The puppies learn to walk on a leash.

The dogs go back to school when they are about one year old.

Trainers teach the dogs to help people who cannot see.

Guide dogs meet their new partners. They get to know each other.

Guide dogs help their partners in many ways. They help their partners cross the street safely.

Guide dogs go where their partners go. They even go to work with their partners!

Words to Know

guide dog

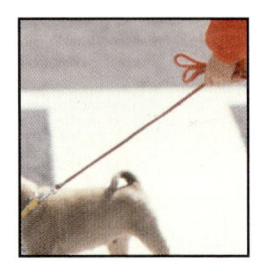

leash

partners

puppy

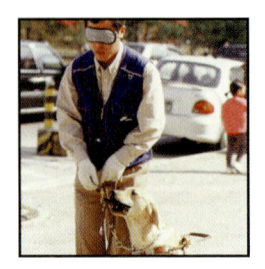

trainer